I0813823

SUPER CUTE!
Baby
Skunks
by Megan Borgert-Spaniol
BLASTOFF! READERS
1
BELLWETHER MEDIA • MINNEAPOLIS, MN

Note to Librarians, Teachers, and Parents:

Blastoff! Readers are carefully developed by literacy experts and combine standards-based content with developmentally appropriate text.

Level 1 provides the most support through repetition of high-frequency words, light text, predictable sentence patterns, and strong visual support.

Level 2 offers early readers a bit more challenge through varied simple sentences, increased text load, and less repetition of high-frequency words.

Level 3 advances early-fluent readers toward fluency through increased text and concept load, less reliance on visuals, longer sentences, and more literary language.

Level 4 builds reading stamina by providing more text per page, increased use of punctuation, greater variation in sentence patterns, and increasingly challenging vocabulary.

Level 5 encourages children to move from "learning to read" to "reading to learn" by providing even more text, varied writing styles, and less familiar topics.

Whichever book is right for your reader, Blastoff! Readers are the perfect books to build confidence and encourage a love of reading that will last a lifetime!

This edition first published in 2017 by Bellwether Media, Inc.

Library of Congress Cataloging-in-Publication Data

Names: Borgert-Spaniol, Megan, 1989- , author.
Title: Baby Skunks / by Megan Borgert-Spaniol.
Description: Minneapolis, MN : Bellwether Media, Inc., 2017. | Series: Blastoff! Readers. Super Cute! | Includes bibliographical references and index. | Audience: Ages 5 to 8. | Audience: Grades K to 3.
Identifiers: LCCN 2016032029 (print) | LCCN 2016038137 (ebook) | ISBN 9781626175471 (hardcover : alk. paper) | ISBN 9781681032764 (ebook)
Subjects: LCSH: Skunks–Infancy–Juvenile literature.
Classification: LCC QL737.C248 B67 2017 (print) | LCC QL737.C248 (ebook) | DDC 599.76/81392–dc23
LC record available at https://lccn.loc.gov/2016032029

Editor: Betsy Rathburn Designer: Brittany McIntosh

Printed in the United States of America, North Mankato, MN.

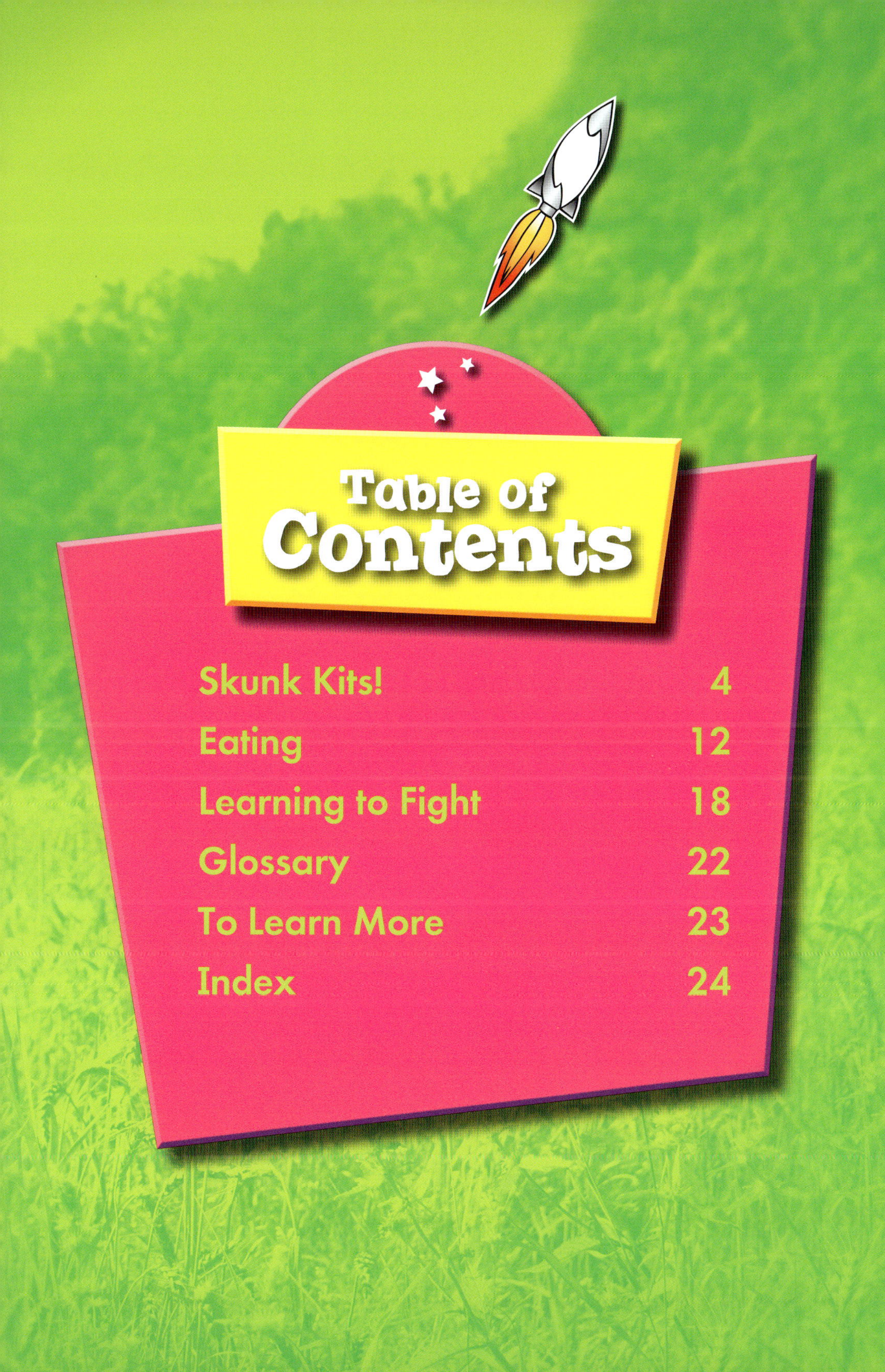

Table of Contents

Skunk Kits!	4
Eating	12
Learning to Fight	18
Glossary	22
To Learn More	23
Index	24

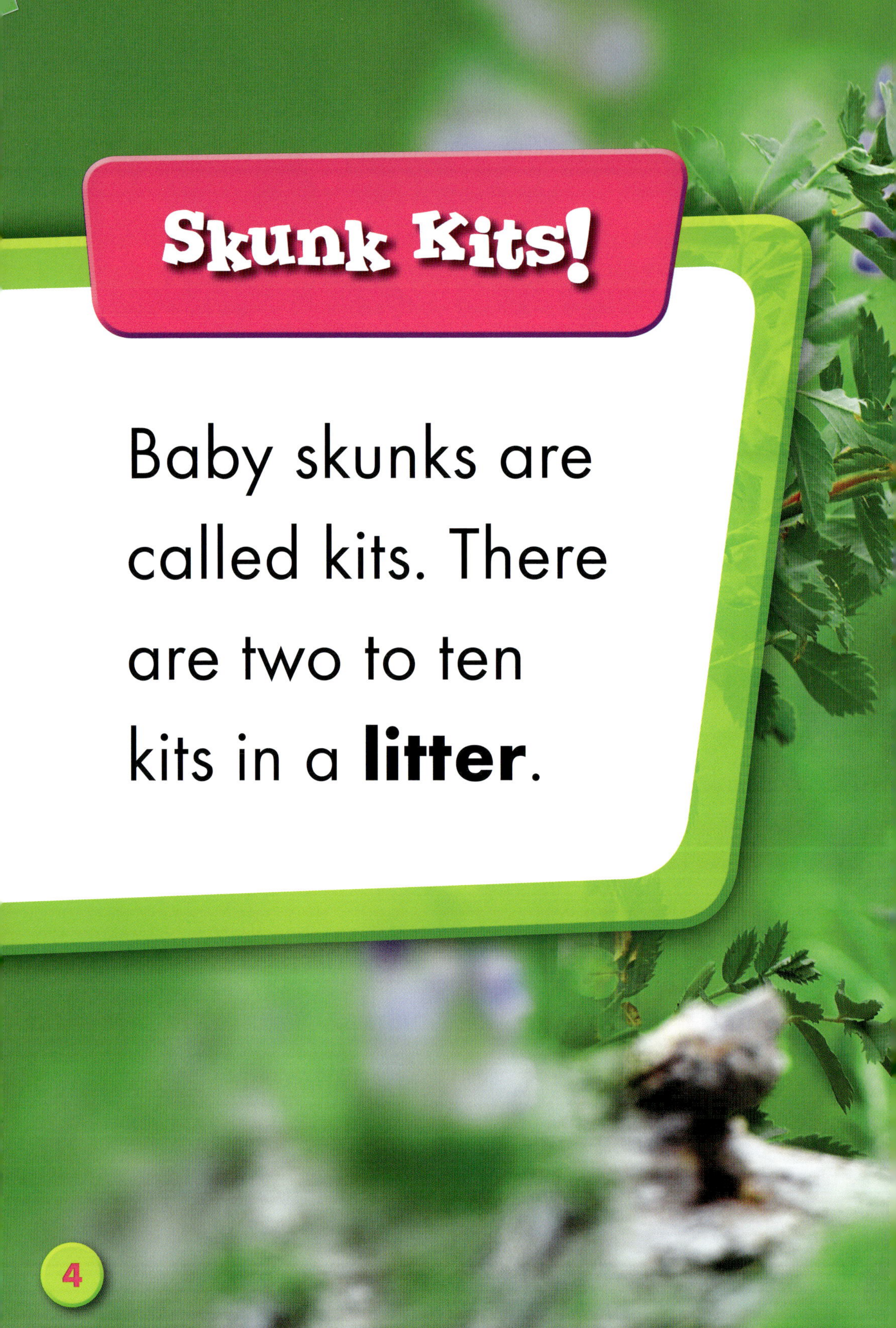

Skunk Kits!

Baby skunks are called kits. There are two to ten kits in a **litter**.

Newborn kits cannot see. They cuddle together in a **den**.

Mom stays close to her babies. She protects them from owls and other **predators**.

Sometimes she carries the kits in her mouth.

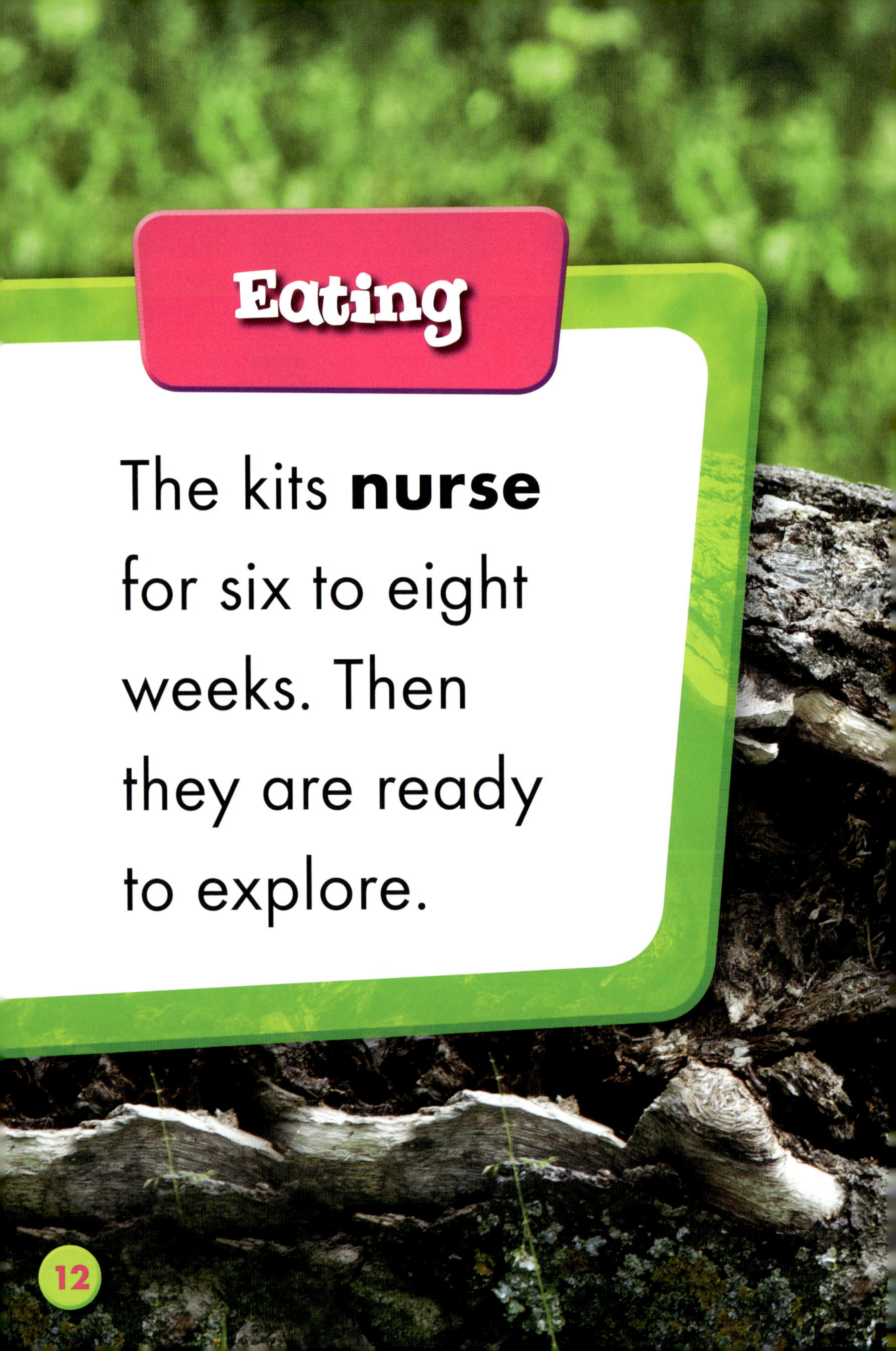

Eating

The kits **nurse** for six to eight weeks. Then they are ready to explore.

They follow mom in a line. She teaches them to find food.

The kits hunt mostly at night. They eat eggs, fruits, and **insects**.

Learning to Fight

The kits learn to protect themselves. They **wrestle** and play for practice.

They also learn to lift their tails and **spray**. The stink keeps predators away!

Glossary

den—the place where skunk kits are born and raised

insects—small animals with six legs and hard outer bodies; an insect's body is divided into three parts.

litter—a group of babies that are born together

newborn—just recently born

nurse—to drink mom's milk

predators—animals that hunt other animals for food

spray—to release a smelly liquid from underneath the tail; skunks spray to defend themselves.

wrestle—to fight in a playful way

To Learn More

AT THE LIBRARY

Green, Emily K. *Skunks*. Minneapolis, Minn.: Bellwether Media, 2011.

Owen, Ruth. *Skunk Kits*. New York, N.Y.: Bearport Pub., 2011.

Whitehouse, Patricia. *Skunks*. Chicago, Ill.: Heinemann Library, 2010.

ON THE WEB

Learning more about skunks is as easy as 1, 2, 3.

1. Go to www.factsurfer.com.
2. Enter "skunks" into the search box.
3. Click the "Surf" button and you will see a list of related web sites.

With factsurfer.com, finding more information is just a click away.

Index

carries, 10
cuddle, 6
den, 6
eat, 16
eggs, 16
explore, 12
follow, 14
food, 14
fruits, 16
hunt, 16
insects, 16
learn, 18, 20
litter, 4
mom, 8, 14
mouth, 10
newborn, 6
night, 16
nurse, 12
play, 18
predators, 8, 20
protects, 8, 18
spray, 20
stink, 20
tails, 20
teaches, 14
wrestle, 18

The images in this book are reproduced through the courtesy of: critterbiz, front cover; Minden Pictures/ SuperStock, pp. 4-5; Papilio/ Alamy, pp. 6-7; Bildagentur Zoonar GmbH, pp. 8-9; Michelle Gilders/ Alamy, pp. 10-11; Debbie Steinhausser, pp. 12-13; Don Johnston/ Glow Images, pp. 14-15; Berquist, Paul & Joyce/ Animals Animals, pp. 16-17; Betty4240, pp. 18-19; Sohns/ imagebroker/ SuperStock, pp. 20-21.